To Bob
w/thanks

HOLDING HEAVEN

A NOVELLA

JERRY B. JENKINS

PAINTINGS BY RON DiCIANNI

HOLDING HEAVEN

A NOVELLA

Published by Integrity Publishers, a division of Integrity Media, Inc.,
5250 Virginia Way, Suite 110, Brentwood, TN 37027.

HELPING PEOPLE WORLDWIDE EXPERIENCE the MANIFEST PRESENCE of GOD.

Jerry B. Jenkins is published in association with Vigliano Associates, Ltd., 405 Park Avenue, Suite 1700, New York, NY 10022.

Ron DiCianni is represented by and this work was produced with assistance from Tapestry Productions Inc, 43980 Mahlon Vail Circle Ste. 803, Temecula, CA 92592.
To see more of Ron DiCianni's artwork please visit: www.TapestryProductions.com

We gratefully acknowledge The Livingstone Corporation for their assistance in this project.

Cover Design: Brand Navigation, LLC – DeAnna Pierce, Bill Chiaravalle, www.brandnavigation.com
Cover Illustration: Ron DiCianni
Interior Design: Susan Browne Design

Library of Congress Cataloging-in-Publication Data

Jenkins, Jerry B.
  Holding heaven / written by Jerry B. Jenkins ; illustrated by Ron DiCianni.
    p. cm.
  Summary: "Story told in novella format between a father and son, Joseph and Christ, of what has happened and what is to come"—Provided by publisher.
  ISBN 1-59145-218-X
  1. Joseph, Saint--Fiction. 2. Jesus Christ--Fiction. I. Title.
  PS3560.E485H65 2005
  813'.54--dc22
                              2005012160

Printed in the United States of America
05 06 07 08 RRD 9 8 7 6 5 4 3 2 1

ACKNOWLEDGMENTS

With thanks to:
Kirk Cameron, who originally sparked the idea
for this book. I owe you one . . .

Integrity Publishers, specifically Joey Paul, who caught
the vision and embraced it as his own.

Livingstone, specifically my friend,
Dave Veerman, who unselfishly put many of the pieces
of this together. Your reward will surely come someday.

Jerry, for even listening to my concept for this book,
let alone for hitting it out of the park.

And most of all . . . to the One who lived it.
There would be no story to write without You.

- Ron DiCianni

MOONLIGHT SOLILOQUY

THE WORKER OF WOOD LAY
ON HIS BACK IN THE DARKNESS, HANDS
BEHIND HIS HEAD, LEATHERY FINGERS
INTERLACED, ONE THROBBING. HIS YOUNG
WIFE SLUMBERED TO HIS LEFT, HER BREATH-
ING EVEN AND DEEP. AN ARM'S LENGTH
FROM HER THE BABY HAD BEGUN TO STIR.
AGAIN.

Such a strange child. Only months old now, the boy never slept through the night. When he finally did drift off, his eyes seemed clamped shut, his moist lips tightened in a scowl. Hungry or wet, he would awaken and cry like any other child.

The man's wife tended to him gently, efficiently, at any hour of the night, and then slipped back into sleep. Reaching for the boy, she would cradle him to her bosom, care for his needs, and whisper him back to sleep.

But Joseph knew it was the baby's other crying, his unfathomable, ethereal sadness, that wore on her. These sounds came inexplicably, even when he was fed and dry and warm, the cotton-filled cloth smooth beneath him, resting on a slightly raised wooden frame fashioned by the carpenter himself to keep the three of them inches from the earthen floor.

Neither Joseph nor his wife could predict when the distress would begin. Though they took turns trying to comfort the child, Joseph sensed Mary's pain, the distraction that robbed her of her rest.

First, the boy would turn, and a squeak would escape his throat. His parents, both light sleepers, would rouse to watch in the moonlight. Mary would draw a tiny blanket to the neck of the swaddled baby and coo his name.

"Jesus."

As she caressed Him, Joseph wanted to cover his own ears to block the mournful sobs sure to follow. At times like this, usually deep into the Egyptian desert night, the boy began to groan, to moan, to give voice to some pain so deep it produced wails without tears.

It was Joseph's turn. The humming had begun, the sad, yearning whine. Mary's breathing changed.

"I'm awake," he whispered.

"I'm sorry, Joseph. He's fed and dry."

He shushed her and sat up. As if the wonder and the terror of the last year had not been enough, his right index finger pulsed with pain. That morning while planing a huge plank in his temporary shop, he had driven a sliver so deeply into the knuckle that he believed it had struck the bone.

Mary had dug out the wood with a needle, cleansed and packed the wound with ointment, and wrapped it with cloth. Soon, though, Joseph found the wrap a nuisance and removed it. Though he tried to favor the pierced finger the rest of the day, he had continued working and paid for it now. The knuckle was swollen nearly twice its normal size, the finger stiff.

Jesus had begun the sob of the forlorn, and Joseph gently pressed a hand to Mary's side to keep her from rising. He could not have chosen a better wife had it been left to him alone. He stood slowly, stretching, his shoulders and biceps tight, thighs bearing deep aches, the pain in his hand outweighing all.

Joseph stepped over his wife and knelt before the child. Blocking the light from the moon, he could not at first see the dainty face. As his eyes grew accustomed to the dark, he was able to make out the tiny, writhing form. He pulled the blanket away and slid his good hand under the baby's gathered nightshirt, covering the heaving belly and torso with his palm, his breath catching at the feathery softness of skin newer than the full moon.

That baby's body was the most pliant thing Joseph touched every day. His thick calluses didn't seem to bother the boy. In fact, the warmth of his hand always seemed to at least temporarily distract Jesus.

The little one calmed, luminous dark eyes darting in the low light until they stopped on Joseph's face. The carpenter imagined that he looked like a black shape silhouetted in the moonlight, and yet it seemed Jesus looked directly into his eyes.

The baby drew in a long breath, and Joseph knew the otherworldly anguish was not over. With his free hand he groped for a thick shawl and slung it over his shoulders, wincing as the material caught the gash at his knuckle.

As Jesus began the pitiful moaning that would lead to more crying, Mary stirred. "Sleep," Joseph said. "I'm going to walk with Him."

"Be sure He's—"

"I will," the carpenter said. He straightened the baby's clothes and enfolded Him fully in the blanket, then gathered the sad infant to his chest and rose.

"Thank you, Joseph," Mary said, her words slurred to where he believed she might actually go back to sleep. How she needed that.

Padding barefoot to his shop, the baby tucked snugly in the crook of his elbow, Joseph found a kidskin bottle draped over his work bench and managed to hold it aloft so he could direct a thin stream of lukewarm water to his tongue. He brushed the foreleg of the skin to Jesus' lips, but the baby turned from it.

"Very well, little one," Joseph said. "Some fresh air, perhaps."

He straightened the baby's blanket to block any draft. Slipping into his cypress-soled leather sandals, he stepped outside. He enfolded the boy with both arms now, shielding Him from the faintest hint of a breeze, and mounted the steps to the rooftop.

Joseph held Jesus so He could see the moon and stars and the gnarled fingers of olive tree branches huddling in the shadows. The baby squirmed, and Joseph feared He would begin wailing anew. "Isn't it beautiful?" he whispered.

Jesus seemed to settle at the sound of Joseph's voice. "So, You want me to talk, do You?"

Joseph moved to a small chair he had fashioned from the remains of a failed oxen yoke project. He used a foot to pull it away from the fortified wall, surprised at its heaviness. He settled with his back to the moonlight and sat the baby on his lap facing him, his dark, smooth face illuminated. The moon and stars reflected in the boy's eyes as He seemed to study Joseph.

"I cannot imagine Your feeling more like my own flesh," Joseph said.

He fell silent, loving the child, until Jesus grew restless again. "Only this tired voice will still You?" Joseph said, smiling, and the baby settled. "Very well, then. What shall I tell You?"

Little one, Your mother and I were very much in love. She had been selected for me, yes. But let me say I was more than somewhat involved in my father's thinking and was pleased with his choice. Your mother and I had grown to know and long for each other, anticipating the day we could be together forever.

Our fathers finalized the contract, and I spent many evenings after my work day fashioning beautiful works of art as gifts to my beloved. We were officially promised to each other at a ceremony in her home. Oh, precious one, You should have seen her! The wait for the actual marriage ceremony, a year hence—seemed a millennium to us.

Joseph smiled at the memory of his beautiful bride-to-be. The baby seemed to be listening, to be taking in His father's words. He pressed His feathery lips together in the moonlight, eyes wide and locked on Joseph's own.

We lived in Palestine; a dwelling place of God's chosen people. The north, Nazareth, was our home. The Roman Empire had occupied us for more than fifty years, establishing an evil king, Herod, to rule over us. But like my countrymen, I was raised under the teaching of the Holy Books, wee one, and like everyone else, I longed for the day when we would again have a voice in our own affairs, as our forefathers did in the days of the great King David.

The Scriptures foretold of a deliverer, and the prophet Malachi prophesied a forerunner, someone to prepare us for that deliverer. That forerunner, my son, is a relative of Yours. Can You believe it?

Your mother's cousin, Elisabeth, is

married to an old priest named Zacharias. They live south of Nazareth and Samaria in the hills of Judah, not far from the temple in Jerusalem. The story, as Your mother told me, is that Zacharias was in the holy place of the temple, it being his turn to offer incense on the altar. Being childless and having given up hope of having a son succeed him as a priest, still he considered this the greatest day of his life.

Jesus blinked slowly, and Joseph felt the little body begin to relax.

"I am boring You, am I not?"

Joseph pulled the nightclothes and blanket tighter, holding the infant closer, but the boy squirmed to keep His face in the moonlight. Joseph stood and moved toward the stairs, but Jesus twisted in his arms all the more.

"And so I must remain seated?" he said. "And You wish me to continue?" Joseph studied the baby's face.

Intent. Attentive. He shook his head. "Some would think me mad, sitting here in the darkness telling stories to an infant . . ."

When Elisabeth later opened the door to her husband at home, she immediately knew something was wrong. He could not speak! He wrote on a tablet to tell her what had happened. While in the temple, an angel had spoken to him—and not just any angel, no, but Gabriel himself, telling Zacharias that Elisabeth would bear a son. They were to call him John, and he would prepare God's people for the long-promised deliverer.

Imagine! An angel speaking to a man! It hadn't happened for centuries. And yet Elisabeth, a godly woman, immediately believed her husband's report. She asked Zacharias why he could not speak, and he wrote that he had at first doubted the

message. Gabriel had stricken him mute
until the promise came true.

Joseph sighed. He was weary, and the breeze had
stiffened. If it made him shudder, surely the baby
was cold. Yet as he again tried to hold Jesus closer
or shift as if to stand, the tiny body struggled afresh
and Joseph settled. He pressed two fingers gently
against the boy's forehead. He seemed warm enough
for now.

Joseph was suddenly overcome. "I will love You
and protect You for as long as I live," he said. "I shall
never let any harm come to You."

The baby continued to focus on him, and Joseph
continued.

Your mother and I often saw each other
at the end of the day, strolling in the
twilight, enjoying dinner at her parents'
home. That's why I was caught off guard
one morning while hard at work. The sun

was stifling, and I could not seem to move any air into my shop. Woodchips flew everywhere. I had to loosen the top of my garment and let it hang at my waist, and soon sawdust found its way to the sweat on my chest and arms.

Oh, little one, I was so embarrassed when I heard the sweet voice of my beloved! I called out for her to wait a moment, quickly brushed myself off, and covered myself fully again.

"I'm so sorry to interrupt you, Joseph," she said, "but I am going to visit my cousin Elisabeth in Judah for a few months and wanted you to know."

I was alarmed. Her plan was to go alone! We were not yet living together as husband and wife, so I couldn't accompany her. All I could do was pray for her safety. How relieved I was when word came that she had arrived safely.

She stayed with her cousin three months, almost to the time of John's birth. When Your mother finally returned, we had a joyous reunion that did not last long. Something was different about her. How shall I say it? She seemed more mature, and somehow both serene and distracted at the same time.

I soon found out why. She told me she had visited her cousin after an angel had told her of Elisabeth's pregnancy. Now, hear me, son, my own father Jacob was named after a dreamer—a man of old who wrestled with an angel and dreamt of a ladder from heaven. I myself was named after an interpreter of dreams. But this news troubled me.

She told me the story of Zacharias and his angelic visit, Elisabeth's pregnancy, John's impending birth. I was stunned. A relative of my fiancée carrying the forerunner of Israel's Messiah? While I knew Your mother would never lie to me and that Elisabeth must indeed be with child, I frankly did not know what to think of all the rest.

But that was not all. In fact, that was the least of it.

I felt like Zacharias—struck dumb—when Your mother told me she herself was with child. My mind raged with questions, with consequences. What was she saying? She, a betrothed woman, had left me for three months and come back pregnant?

Let me tell You, little one: it was a blessing from the Almighty that I was unable to utter a sound. Nothing that came to mind would have done anything but cause pain. She rushed to assure me she had been pregnant before she left for Judah and that, of course, she had not been unfaithful to me.

But what was I to think? I was trying to fathom Zacharias's story of an angelic visit, and now Your mother was telling me . . . what? That the same angel, Gabriel, had visited her, even before she knew Zacharias's story!

I was shuddering, my eyes filling; no doubt my face was flushed. Your mother put a hand on my arm, but I could not respond.

"Joseph, hear me," she whispered with such urgency that I had to listen. "Gabriel greeted me and told me the Lord was with me. You cannot begin to imagine my fear, but he told me not to be frightened, because God had chosen to bless me. He told me I was to have a son and to name Him Jesus; that He would be great and called the Son of the Most High. God was to give Him the throne of David and He would rule over Israel forever!

"I know what you're thinking, Joseph, and I asked the same question. How could I have a child when I am a virgin? Gabriel told me that God's Holy Spirit would come upon me and that the power of the Most High would overshadow me. The baby would be the holy Son of God."

I opened my mouth, but still could not speak. Your mother was pregnant, and now this strange story! But I loved her! How could I end our betrothal while keeping her from shame and perhaps even death?

"Joseph, the angel also told me that Elisabeth, despite her advanced age, was six months pregnant because nothing is impossible with God. What could I say? I believed. I am the Lord's servant and willing to serve Him in any way He asks."

Aah, child, to my shame I rose to leave her sitting there, but she was not finished.

"When I arrived in Judah," she said, "Elisabeth told me that the child within her leapt. She told me that my child and I were blessed, and she called me the mother of her Lord."

All I could do was shake my head. It was too much. I longed to believe her, yet I am but a man. I tried to work, but my hands were worthless. By the middle of another hot afternoon I had much to accomplish, but I had to stop. I staggered to my mat and sat with my head in my hands. What could I do? The last thing I wanted was for Your mother to suffer.

Soon I lay back and fell asleep, and child, as God is my witness, an angel visited me in a dream. From the first instant, I knew it was real. He called me by my name and identified me as a son of David. He told me not to be afraid to marry Your mother, because You were indeed conceived by the Holy Spirit. He told me she would have a son and that I was to name Him Jesus, for He would save His people from their sins.

When I awoke, I never looked back. I knew the ancient texts. Since my childhood I had heard the prophecy that a virgin would conceive a son who would be called Immanuel, or "God is with us." That, my son, as wondrous as it is to even imagine, is You.

The baby grew restless in his arms, so Joseph stood and moved to the edge of the roof, drawing the boy close to his chest.

Your mother was from a godly family, of course, people who knew and honored the ancient texts. No angels visited them, but I believe it was God Himself who led them to accept our accounts. They agreed we should marry immediately. How proud I was, during the ceremony, to proclaim to all, "She is my wife and I her husband, from today and forever."

You can only imagine how slowly the next half year moved. As You grew within her, I came to love You as if You were my own. Your mother and I talked and talked long into the night, every night, still wondering at the unfathomable privilege and responsibility God had bestowed upon us.

Though I had known Your mother to be uncommonly devoted to God and the Holy Scriptures, who would have ever dreamed that my wife would be chosen for such a singular role? As for me, frankly, I may never shed my feeling of unworthiness. To serve as her husband, to be Your earthly father, to be so honored as to be assigned to name You, my child and my Savior . . .

Night after night, when we expressed our thanks and devotion to God, Your mother repeated this until it burned itself into my mind:

"Oh, how I praise the Lord. How I rejoice in God my Savior! For He took notice of His lowly servant girl, and now generation after generation will call me blessed.

"For He, the Mighty One, is holy, and He has done great things for me. His mercy goes on from generation to genera-tion, to all who fear Him.

"His mighty arm does tremendous things! How He scatters the proud and haughty ones! He has taken princes from their thrones and exalted the lowly.

"He has satisfied the hungry with good things and sent the rich away with empty hands. And how He has helped His servant Israel! He has not forgotten His promise to be merciful.

"For He promised our ancestors—Abraham and his children—to be merciful to them forever."

Joseph moved to the stairs and gingerly descended, peeking in at Mary as he moved around to the back of the house. She appeared to sleep soundly.

As Joseph reached a tiny cypress grove, the baby twisted in what seemed an attempt to keep His eyes on the sky. When Joseph resumed speaking, the boy's eyes found his again.

We were excited as the time came near for Your birth. All the preparations had been made; the midwife prepared to visit us at first notice. And then came the news. We had to go to Bethlehem for registration and taxing. I might have been able to secure an exception for Your mother,

her delivery time being so near, but we were not willing to be apart. To the very last moment, we debated the wisdom of such a trip, nearly seventy miles over several days, but Your mother insisted.

With the counsel of the midwife in my ears, we set out. I walked the entire way. Your mother alternated walking and riding a small donkey. More than once I regretted bringing her, but despite the pain in her eyes, she never complained.

I myself was bone weary when we finally reached Bethlehem late one chilly night. Your mother tried to keep from me her whimpers and winces at every step, but all she wanted was to stop and rest. When the first innkeeper we approached told us his inn was full, I pleaded our case, telling him my wife was great with child.

"I must find lodging immediately," I told him. "Where would you suggest?"

"Oh, sir," he said, "we have sought makeshift accommodations for others already. There is not a room to be found in the city tonight."

"I'll take anything. A corner somewhere. Just get us out of the weather."

He looked past me, avoiding Your mother's eyes, then looked behind him. Finally his gaze settled on me. "Follow me," he said. "This is wholly up to you."

He led me through an alley behind his inn and into a stable where his tenants' animals were kept. It was dank and smelly and cold. My shoulders drooped, and I lowered my head. What was I to do? This was no place for a pregnant woman.

I shook my head, about to tell the man this would never do, but Your mother touched my arm. "It's shelter," she said. "I must lie down."

The man shrugged. "It's free," he said.

I thanked him, secured the donkey, and grabbed a rake to form a small hay mow for Your mother. She settled painfully, and I pulled from our pack the last of our foodstuffs. I ate heartily but could not get Your mother to eat anything. She told me she feared her time was near.

By the time I spread a rug on the floor and fashioned a bed in the hay for her, Your mother was in labor. She urged me to save enough cloth for the baby. I built a small fire, close enough for warmth, yet near enough to the entrance to give the fire air and keep the smoke away. Soon Your mother was deep into labor, and there was little I could do but hold her hand.

I had had my nervous moments in the past—like the first time my work was judged by my father, a master craftsman—but nothing like this, not ever. Yet when the time came—that is to say, when You came—somehow God was with me. I did what needed to be done, followed the instructions the midwife had sent with me, and soon there You were.

Let me tell You, precious one, You did not appear to have been sent from God. Red and squalling, You should have attracted the attention of the revelers in the crowded streets. But apparently no one heard You but us.

Your mother gently wiped You dry and wrapped You tightly in cloth, enfolding You to her chest to keep You warm. Meanwhile I formed a nest of hay for You in a box made of wood. Soon the rigors of the trip and the labor caught up with Your mother, and she asked me to take You. She could no longer keep her eyes open.

When You settled into my arms, I felt as if I were holding heaven. After You fell asleep and I felt myself drifting, I nestled

You in the manger and pulled it close to where Your mother and I lay. I draped my cloak over her, and she looked as if she could sleep for hours.

I settled back, fatigue finally washing over me. Even more, I was overcome by a love for You that flooded my being.

Not long after, I roused. Your mother already had You in her lap.

"He was hungry," she said.

She was nursing You when I heard conversation in the alley. It would have been futile to ask passersby to keep quiet for Your sake. I'd rather not have drawn attention to the truth that we had a newborn in a stable. But they must have noticed my fire, and perhaps they merely wanted a moment of warmth.

But no. They were looking for something. For someone.

"This has to be the place," one said. I

counted five men and could tell by their garb, and yes, I confess, by their smell, that they were shepherds. In the nearby hills, many tended flocks that would be used for temple sacrifices in Jerusalem five or six miles away.

"Is there a baby here?" they asked.

How could they know? They had not been close enough to see, and You had not so much as whimpered in more than an hour. I didn't know what to say. What was their business? What did they want with You?

"A baby?" I said, determined to protect You. "Why do you ask?"

"Sir," the eldest said earnestly, his face bright with enthusiasm, "we mean no harm. We were tending our flocks outside the village when an angel of the Lord appeared and glory shone all around us. We were scared to death, but he told us not to be afraid. He said he brought us good news of great joy. The Savior, yes, the Messiah, the Lord, has been born tonight in Bethlehem. He said we would find the baby in a manger, wrapped snugly in strips of cloth."

What could I do? I stepped aside and motioned for them to come in. Your mother was settling You in the manger again, and she welcomed the strangers as if she had expected them. They knelt before You, thanking God. One told their story to her:

"Suddenly the whole sky was full of angels, saying, 'Glory to God in the highest heaven, and peace on earth to all whom God favors.'"

She merely smiled. And when they finally left, we could hear them telling everyone. People began finding their way into the alley and past the stable, saying,

"Is it true? Is it true? Is that the Messiah?"

I could not envision a way to return to Nazareth with a newborn, and so after our business was conducted the next day, I set about finding lodging. Although rooms remained scarce, I was able to secure a home for two months. That would give Your mother time to regain her strength, and allow us to have You circumcised and named after eight days. After the time of purification, we could present You to the Lord at the temple in Jerusalem.

During the next thirty-three days, during the purification rite for Your mother, occasional pilgrims would find our home and ask to see You. The word was spreading because of the shepherds, who were still apparently telling what they had seen.

Finally the day came—forty-one days after You were born—for us to take You to the temple to present You to the Lord with a gift of two turtledoves. The words caught in my throat, but I forced myself to be heard, to say them just the way the angel told me.

"His name is to be Jesus," I said, "for He shall save His people from their sins."

While we were there, our hearts full and wondering how the Lord God would respond to the very child He had sent, two very strange events occurred.

The baby blinked slowly, and Joseph yawned. The boy had seemed fascinated by his voice, but now both were flagging. Joseph leaned against a tree and shifted the baby. "Time to return to Your bed?"

The child stared at him and sighed.

"You'll be hungry soon, son," he said. "Meanwhile, I shall continue."

We presented You and the turtledoves to the priest, and as soon as the brief ceremony concluded, we went to retrieve our donkey and a bit of lunch. But an old man approached with a weary smile.

"Forgive me," he said, "but may I hold your son?"

I looked to Your mother, willing to follow her wishes, but she was already putting You in his arms. The man introduced himself as Simeon, a local resident who had been praying for years for the Messiah who would come and rescue Israel.

His voice thick with emotion, he told us, "God's Holy Spirit revealed to me I would not die until I saw the Lord's Christ. He led me here today, to you, to this child."

He held You aloft and praised God, saying, "Lord, now I can die in peace! As You promised me, I have seen the Savior You have given to all people. He is a light to reveal You to the nations, and He is the glory of Your people Israel!"

Simeon gave us his blessing and said to Your mother, "This child will be rejected by many in Israel, and it will be their un-doing. But He will be the greatest joy to many others. Thus the deepest thoughts of many hearts will be revealed. And a sword shall pierce His very soul."

He thanked us as he handed You back, but You can imagine how that last state-ment clouded our joy. We knew the Scrip-tures, of course. We knew the prophecies said You would suffer at the hands of men. In spite of that, I resolved anew to allow no harm to come to You for as long as God gave me breath.

An old prophetess, a woman named Anna, came to us as Simeon was talk-ing with us. People told us she was in her eighties, a widow who never left the temple but stayed there day and night, worshiping God with fasting and prayer.

"This is Jesus!" she proclaimed to pass-ersby. "This is the one we have all been waiting for, the promised King who shall deliver Jerusalem!"

Shortly after we returned to our tempo-rary home in Bethlehem, we were visited by exotic men from the east. They were wise magi who brought You gifts, gold and frankincense and myrrh. They bowed low to worship You and spoke urgently and quietly among themselves.

Then one told me they had been fol-lowing a star for nearly two years before Your birth to find You. When they had gotten as far as Jerusalem, they began ask-ing, "Where is the newborn King of the Jews? We have come to worship Him."

He told me they had been summoned to the court of King Herod.

"The king said he had called a meeting

of the leading priests and teachers of religious law and had asked them where the prophets said the Messiah would be born. They quoted Micah, who wrote, 'O Bethlehem of Judah, you are not just a lowly village in Judah, for a ruler will come from you who will be the shepherd for my people Israel.'"

I asked him, "So, King Herod knows of Jesus?"

"He seemed troubled by the news," the wise man told me. "He told us to go to Bethlehem and search for the child, and when we found Him, come back and tell him so he can worship the new king too. We followed the star to this very place."

Son, I have never trusted King Herod, and it troubled me that he was aware of You. I did not believe he meant to worship You, but I didn't know what to do. I told

Your mother that we might have to head home to Nazareth sooner than we had planned.

But that very night an angel of God visited me as I dreamt and told me, "Get up and flee to Egypt with the child and His mother. Stay there until I tell you to return, because Herod is going to try to kill the child."

I woke Your mother and we left that instant, hurriedly packing our belongings and stealing away in the night. When we finally arrived here in Egypt three days later, we were out of King Herod's juris-diction. I had to borrow tools to set up my shop. How we long for the day when we can return home to Nazareth.

The baby stretched, His tiny fists pressed against Joseph's nightclothes.

"I need to sit again, little one. I'll finish my story on the rooftop and then we'll see if it's time for Your mother to feed You, hmm?"

Joseph moved around the house again and slowly mounted the steps. The wind was stiffer now, but it was more than the cold that made him shiver.

This is the saddest part of our story, child. Your story. Word soon came from Jerusalem that King Herod was furious. The men from the east never returned to tell him where they had found You, and, of course, by the time he sent soldiers to seek You out, we were gone. In a fit of rage he ordered that all male children in Bethlehem—more than two dozen—be put to death. The massacre has become known as the Slaughter of the Innocents. How we thank God that You were spared, but how we grieve for those who lost their precious little ones!

This, too, of course, had been prophesied centuries before. The prophet Jer-
emiah wrote, "A cry of anguish is heard
in Ramah—weeping and mourning unre-
strained. Rachel weeps for her children,
refusing to be comforted—for they are
dead."

Joseph sat again on the wood bench, setting the
child on his lap, facing him. He reached under the
blanket and allowed the boy to grasp his index
fingers and hold Himself up. The diminutive face
was animated, the lips pressed together, and Joseph
feared the hungry baby would begin crying again.
He tried to hush Him, but the infant groaned and
pitched forward, nodding as if falling asleep.

A low moan escaped Him, and He released
His grip on Joseph's fingers. The carpenter quickly
reached behind the boy to gather Him up, standing
and straightening the blanket and nightclothes. He

pulled the boy to his chest, the tiny cheek pressed against his shoulder.

And as he carefully descended the steps, Joseph realized his finger felt suddenly whole. No pain. No swelling. He turned in the darkness and held it toward the moonlight. No wound.

Joseph slipped out of his sandals at the door and tiptoed to the bedroom, carefully lowering the boy to the mat beside Mary. She roused. "He must be hungry," she said.

"Sleeping," Joseph whispered, covering the baby and stretching out beside his wife.

When he heard the boy stir, he rolled up onto one elbow and peered past Mary. Jesus had fought free from His blanket and lay in the moonlight on His back, arms outstretched, feet crossed at the ankles. Joseph studied Him, a coldness finding its way through his chest.

When the baby cried out, Mary drew Him to her chest and whispered as she nursed Him.

Joseph lay back down, idly rubbing his healed knuckle with his thumb. He quickly drifted off, but in a dream, he was sitting up, a brilliant light filling the room. He was alone, except for an angel of the Lord.

"Take the child and His mother back to the land of Israel," the angel said, "because those who were trying to kill the child are dead."

DEATHBED CONVERSATION

Nearing the thirtieth anniversary of His birth, Jesus has again worked until dusk. He strives to accomplish the work of two men, keeping up with the demand for wood wheels, saddle pieces, sandal soles, oxen yokes, ploughs, and the like. Though of only average height, He is lean and sinewy, His torso solid, arms and shoulders taut from hard, daily physical labor.

Wearing His father's ancient wood-soled sandals and carrying a pot under one arm and a ragged cloth towel draped over the other, He has walked less than half a mile to the only well in Nazareth. He waits in the shadows as two young women laugh and talk, finishing their drawing of water. When they are gone, He makes sure no one else is about, hurries to the well, disrobes to His loincloth, and lowers the community bucket deep into the water.

Hauling it up thrice, He pours it into His pot each time until full. He brushes the wood chips and sawdust from His hair, beard, chest, and arms. Then He hefts the heavy pot above His head and dumps half of it over Himself, bracing against the cool liquid in the twilight.

Jesus vigorously wipes Himself down, then empties the pot over Himself, finally toweling off. As He pulls His garment back on He hears a familiar voice.

"Son?"

He wrings out the towel. "Yes, Mother. Is he—?"

"He's asking for You."

Jesus hurriedly fills His pot again. "Coming," He says, and lifting the vessel, joins her. "Is he lucid?"

"He is. Very weak. Very tired."

Jesus nods. "Is he in pain?"

"No doubt, but he will not complain."

"What does he want of Me? Is it the end?"

"Who can know?" she says. "He wants to talk."

Jesus smiles. "He wants to listen."

His mother shakes her head as they hurry along. "Coming to find You reminds me of when You were twelve."

"I remember."

"We were worried sick."

"At first you weren't."

She shrugs. "We assumed You were with friends."

"I was! New friends."

"Adults! Men of the temple! Scholars. Merely a child, and You had them astonished."

"I was merely asking questions."

"Questions with sharp points."

"You were angry with Me, Mother."

"You admonished me! Said I should know where You would be, that You would be in Your Father's house, about His business."

Jesus drapes an arm around her shoulders. "And so I was."

Back at the cramped house, the aroma of fresh hewn cypress, pomegranate wood, olive wood, and even some rare and expensive cedar wafting from the attached shop, Jesus carried a heavy chair to His father's bedside as His mother poured a cup of water from the pot. "I'll be nearby," she said.

Joseph was dozing noisily. Jesus prayed silently, *Father, Your will be done. I shall miss him, but I thank You for him.*

When Joseph roused, Jesus carefully held the cup to his lips. "My son," the old man said.

"My father."

"The accounts? The orders?"

"Rest," Jesus said. "Everything is on schedule and under control."

"Because of You," Joseph said.

Jesus chuckled. "Because of you. The shop could run itself for years."

Joseph shook his head but did not respond. Finally he managed, "You have been a good son. So beloved. So respected."

"All I want is to honor you and My heavenly Father."

Joseph grimaced and looked troubled. Though Jesus knew, He said, "Are you in pain?"

"I am troubled, my son. I know the Holy Books. Trouble lies ahead for You, and I am helpless."

"I am no longer your responsibility. I shall do the will of My Father in heaven."

Joseph struggled to push himself up on his elbows.

"Rest, Father. Please."

"I would that no harm should come to You. I want to be Your protector. I—"

"I must fulfill My mission."

"But what does that mean? If You are the chosen one, the deliverer, the ruler of Israel, why must—?"

Jesus set down the cup and lowered Joseph to his back again. "Ours is to do the will of God," He said.

"What is the will of God for You, son? What will happen? What is to come?"

Jesus shook His head. "I will obey. That is all."

Joseph shifted as if uncomfortable. "I will not be able to rest without knowing. Tell me. Please."

The son sighed in the darkness, praying silently His father would sleep. Mary brought in a steaming bowl of lentils with small pieces of dried fish and chunks of cheese. Joseph refused even a bite. "Let the boy eat," he said.

"I can eat later, Father," Jesus said.

"Please. Enjoy this for me, while it's hot."

When Jesus finished, He made Joseph take another sip of water, then drank from the cup Himself. Weary, He wished He could stretch out beside His father.

"If You are to be the ruler of Israel," Joseph said, "why must You suffer? Tell me—when will You take the throne?"

So that was it. His own father misunderstood the

prophecies as well. Jesus would not take the throne in the conventional sense—at least not then, not soon. He knew He had been sent as the sacrificial lamb for the sins of the world. The victory, the triumph, the ransom would come in two parts. The payment for sin first. The ultimate victory for God's chosen people millennia later.

Jesus lowered His head and rubbed His eyes, running a hand through His beard. "It will soon come time for the world to understand who I am," He began.

"Yes, yes," the old man said. "Tell me."

"Abba, you taught Me the customs, the traditions, schooled Me in the Holy Books. You taught Me to fish. You taught Me your trade."

Joseph waved Him off. "Let us not reminisce. I did what any father would do. You were easy. What I want to know is what comes next? What will I miss? How will a carpenter be revealed to the world as having come from God? Who will believe it? Why will they believe it?"

"Many won't."

The old man rolled on his side, facing away from his son. He groaned. "That is my worry. Your pain will be my pain."

"You have done all you can for Me, Father. It has pleased Me to be your son. And now it will please Me to do the will of My Father in heaven."

"What is He asking of You?"

There was no getting beyond it. The old man would not be put off. Generalities would not placate him. "Many wonderful things are to come," Jesus said.

"And many hard things," Joseph said. "If You care for me, if You would still honor me, spare me none of it."

"Very well. I suppose you have been hearing of the preaching of cousin Elisabeth's John."

"I have heard," Joseph said. "They call him the Baptist, but most think him mad. He rants that the kingdom of heaven is at hand; yet he wears ragged clothing, eats food from the wild, and preaches in the wilderness. People from all over go out to hear him. He calls down the religious leaders and even the Romans. He's likely to get himself killed."

When Jesus did not respond, Joseph turned toward Him. "Not to mention the one he preaches about, the one he says will not be baptized with water but with the Holy Spirit and fire. He's foretelling Your coming, is he not?"

Jesus nodded.

"He's going to get You killed as well," Joseph said.

"Nothing will happen that is not the will of God," Jesus said. "When John baptizes Me—"

"Must he?"

"He must, because we must do everything that is right. And when he does, the heavens will be opened and the Spirit of God will descend upon Me, and God will call Me His beloved Son, in whom He is pleased."

"I would trade a year of my life to witness that."

Jesus did not respond.

"I will not be there, will I?"

"No."

The old man covered his face with both hands.

"But you will also be spared My trials," Jesus said. "God will allow the evil one to tempt Me."

"Tempt You how?"

"Lonely and starving, I will be tempted to miraculously turn stones to bread. But we both know people need more than bread, don't we? They need to feed on every word that proceeds from the mouth of God. I will be tempted to leap from the highest point of the temple, forcing God's angels to protect Me. But the Scriptures warn against tempting the Lord God. Then I will be offered the world and all it has to offer if I would but kneel before the devil."

"But You will resist."

"By God's grace, I will command the evil one to leave Me. And then I will set about preaching that the kingdom of God is near and that men and women must repent of their sins and turn to Him."

Joseph ran his hands through his hair. "And this is when You will be rejected? People will view You as a madman, like John before You?"

"Some will. But many will come to repentance. God will bless Me and His people through Me. I am the good news. I come with the message of the kingdom, that the powerless, the meek, the humble, and the poor will be redeemed and lifted up."

Mary stepped in with a candle. "And will you eat now, Joseph?" she said.

He nodded. "A little."

As they waited for his food, Jesus noticed Joseph's eyes shining in the candlelight. He had rallied. "The proud will be brought low," Joseph said. "The weak shall be exalted."

Jesus nodded and smiled. "I have a long road and much to do in a short time."

"And will You be alone?"

"I will not. I will surround myself with a small band of men God has already chosen."

"A cabinet of wise counselors."

Jesus laughed. "Some wiser than others," He said. "Fishermen, mostly. A tax collector. Not the kind one might expect."

"They will help You conquer the enemies of the people of God and ascend to the throne of David?"

Jesus was grateful for His mother's interruption. He took the bowl and fed His father. "They will be my friends," He said. "They will be good and bad, helpful and disappointing. I will teach them."

"And they will be Your advisers when You come into Your kingdom."

A breeze found its way through the window, and Jesus set aside the bowl and pulled the blanket to His father's neck. "Are you not weary? Should you not sleep?"

"There will soon be plenty of time for sleep, my son. Tell me, who will be Your enemies and why will they hate You?"

Jesus sat forward, elbows on His knees, chin in His hands. "The proud, the puffed up, those who would usurp the authority of God will not receive Me. I will preach a message of paradoxes."

"Paradoxes?"

Jesus studied him. The old man's voice sounded

weaker. "Do you want to rest awhile?"

Joseph shook his head. "I want to learn. I want to know."

"The message of heaven is foreign to the minds of men. God's ways are not men's ways."

"God is difficult to understand?"

"He who has ears, let him hear."

"Tell me a paradox of God."

"There are many."

"One."

"Very well. Think about this. Unless a person changes to become like a little child, he will never enter the kingdom of heaven. Whoever humbles himself like a child is the greatest in the kingdom of heaven."

Joseph stared into Jesus' eyes. "I will have to ponder that."

"You see?"

"No. Say it again."

Jesus did.

"Profound," Joseph said.

"Of course. It is the wisdom of God Himself."

"Another."

"Whoever finds his life will lose it, and whoever loses his life for My sake will find it."

Joseph shook his head. "The words fill my brain, and yet . . ."

"Think about it in the morning."

"Morning may not come for me. Tell me more."

As the midnight hour approached, the old carpenter seemed to take a turn for the worse. He lay motionless much of the time, and when words came, they were slurred. He seemed to try to focus on his son, but then his eyes would glaze over and roll back. But just when Jesus thought he was dozing and stopped talking, Joseph would rouse, sometimes opening only one eye.

"Don't leave me," he said. "Talk to me, my son."

"You must rest," Jesus said.

"I am resting. But I must know. Years ago I was visited by angels. Once to tell me of Your birth.

Once to flee the sword of Herod. Once to return to Israel. And finally once to return to Galilee."

"God is still with you," Jesus said.

"I know. I know. With You in our home, it has been like having an angel with us every day. But while God told us You were the chosen one, there is so much we did not know. So much we do not know still. What will become of You?"

Jesus Himself was tired and wished He could stretch out on His own mat and try to rejuvenate His body for the next day. But if His father did not last the night, there would be no work anyway. The shop would be closed. The family would prepare the body. It would fall to Him to care for His mother.

She slipped into the room, looking as tired and old as He had ever seen her. He stood. Fear shone in her eyes. Joseph seemed unaware of her. "Sleeping?" she mouthed, motioning for Jesus to sit again.

Jesus shook His head. "No. Fighting the end."

"You'll send for me . . ." she said, leaving the hard reality unsaid.

"Of course."

Joseph stirred. "I thirst."

Mary fetched the pitcher and Jesus poured. He sat Joseph up as she held the cup to his lips. The old man tried to drink greedily, but he coughed and sputtered and had to lie back. "An entire pitcher would not satisfy me," he said.

"Mother, please," Jesus said. "You, too, must rest. Full, trying days lie ahead."

She cupped His chin in her palm and nodded. When she was gone, Jesus bent close to His father. "Whoever drinks this water will thirst again. But whoever drinks of Me shall never thirst. Let anyone who is thirsty come to Me and drink. For the Scriptures declare that rivers of living water shall flow from the hearts of those who believe in Me."

Joseph turned and squinted in the candlelight, looking Jesus full in the face. "I know who You are," he said. "I believe in You."

"I am the resurrection and the life," Jesus said. "He that believes in Me, though he were dead, yet shall he live. And whoever lives and believes in Me shall never die. Do you believe this?"

Joseph let his head fall back. "I believe You are the Christ, the Son of God come into the world."

"Soon you will be with My Father in paradise."

Joseph grew restless, his head moving side to side.

"Father, are you suffering?"

"No," the old man rasped. "I am bewildered. I know who You are because I was told, and because I have lived with You, lo, these many years. But how will others know? Of course, they will reject You, the son of a carpenter from lowly Galilee. Unless an angel reveals to them the truth, why should they not think You mad if You go about proclaiming that You are the Son of God?"

Jesus began to answer, but His father was not finished.

"Why can You not just prove it? Why must You be rejected and come to harm? Is there no alternative?"

"It has been prophesied."

"But why?"

"It is the will of God."

"I dare not question the will of God, but though You are not of my flesh, still I love You as my own son. If God gave me strength, I would protect You, I would tell the world, I would—"

Jesus laid a hand gently on His father's shoulder. "Many will accept and believe."

"And yet many will not! I—"

"God is not willing that any should perish. That is why He has sent His light into the world, to draw men and women to Himself. I will speak His truth, His message. I will—"

"But that will not be enough! You must prove You are the Son of God!"

"The truth will be there for those who have eyes and ears."

"Because You say it? I myself would call You mad if I didn't know better!"

"I will do the works of God. Those who are not blinded will see."

"What does this mean? What will You do?"

Jesus trimmed the lamp and sighed. "You have been such good parents, taking me to Jerusalem for Passover every year for as long as I could remember."

"Since Your birth," Joseph managed.

Jesus nodded. "I have continued going. And that will not change. I am to be the Passover lamb, and My Father has work for Me in the temple. It has become a den of thieves."

"Den of thieves? Lamb? I am confused. As God's messenger, You have the right to make things right in His house. But how will the authorities know that? Will You call down fire from heaven as the prophets of old?"

Jesus shook His head. "There will be enough evidence for those who need to know."

"Miracles? You will perform miracles?"

Jesus added a blanket to His father's bedclothes. "You must conserve your strength."

"Why?" the old man said. "Do You need my help in the shop tomorrow?" Humor danced in his eyes.

Jesus smiled. "I don't want to see you suffer."

"Heal me." His father was still smiling.

"Nothing would please Me more. Restoring you to youth and vigor and strength would bring glory to God and cause many to believe. That is the only purpose of such acts, to bring many to repentance."

"But then I would not soon be with Your Father in paradise."

"No. And I believe that is His will."

"As do I," Joseph said. "Your mother wishes other-wise, of course."

"Of course. She has asked Me to heal you too. But My time has not yet come."

"When will Your time come?"

"Soon."

Joseph dozed for several minutes. When his eyes flickered open again, he said, "Lamb? Passover lamb? That is how You will save Your people from their sins?"

Jesus merely looked at him.

"Is it the only way?"

"It is God's plan. His will. And that is My mission. To do His will."

"But if You perform miracles, no one will want to harm You!"

"There is a way that seems right to men, but the ends thereof are the ways of death. 'For My thoughts are not your thoughts, neither are your ways My ways,' says the Lord. 'For as the heavens are higher than the earth, so are My ways than your ways, and My thoughts than your thoughts.'"

Joseph rolled on his side again and seemed to sleep. But he said, "It is no surprise to me that men make no sense. But must You die?"

"I must do the will of Him who sent Me."

Facing away from Jesus in the darkness, Joseph moaned. "What message will You bring that will so revile people?"

Jesus stood over His father and kneaded his back. "If we must talk of things to come, let us talk of the joyful things."

"The miracles?"

"If you wish."

"Please."

"I will be imbued with power from on high and given authority over demons and illness and death, even nature. I will heal the sick, give sight to the blind, hearing to the deaf, speech to the mute. I will cast out demons, cleanse the lepers, allow the lame to walk, restore a withered limb, calm a storm, feed hungry masses, raise the dead."

Joseph rolled onto his back and Jesus sat. "How I long to see it," the old man said. "To see it all."

"You would not want to see all of it," Jesus said.

"But those You heal, those You minister to, they would never want to see harm come to You."

"They shall be powerless in the face of God's will."

Joseph struggled to sit up and began to swing his legs off the side of his bed.

"Easy, Father."

"I need to walk."

"You want to walk?"

The old man nodded. "When You were an infant, I walked You in the night. You can do the same for me."

"If you're certain . . ."

"I am."

"Let Me get your staff, and you must wear your cloak."

Jesus left the room and found His mother sleeping. She started. "Is he—"

"He wants to walk."

"Oh! He mustn't!" she said, standing.

"You know as well as I that he will do what he wishes," Jesus said.

When He returned with the long wood stick and His father's cloak, Mary was scolding Joseph. "You're acting the old fool again," she said, but Jesus read bemusement in her tone. "You'll need one of us on either side."

Joseph's brow knitted. Clearly he did not want his wife to hear what he was so desperate to know.

"We'll be well, the boy and I. Just let us be. We won't be out long."

She shook her head as her husband struggled to stand, gripping the staff with both hands. Mary helped him into his cloak. "Cover your head," she said. She turned to Jesus. "Will he be warm enough?"

"I'll see to it. Please try to sleep. We'll be just outside."

Mary had trimmed a lamp and handed it to Jesus as He slowly led His father out. "Promise me You won't be long," she said.

"Try to sleep," He said. "You must stay strong for the days ahead."

Father and son made their way behind the house, and Jesus set the lantern down. Joseph sat and leaned close, grasping his son's robe. "If You bring the message of God and do mighty works in His name, what will turn men against You?"

Jesus spoke softly to be sure He was heard only by

Joseph. "People search the Scriptures because they believe that in them they will find eternal life. But the Scriptures point to Me. Yet they will refuse to come to Me. Their approval or disapproval means nothing to Me, because they will not have God's love within them. They will gladly honor each other, but will not care about the honor that comes from God alone. A prophet is honored everywhere except in his own country. People should spend their energy seeking the eternal life I can give. God the Father has sent Me for that very purpose. God wants people to believe in the one He has sent."

Joseph looked sad. "How will You be able to have patience with such selfishness? How long will You be able to put up with such insolence?"

"I have told you, Father. I have come from heaven to do the will of God who sent Me, not to do what I want. And the will of God is that I should not lose even one of all those He has given Me, but that I should raise them to eternal life at the last day. It is My Father's will that all who see His Son and believe in Him should have eternal life—that I should raise them at the last day."

"Who could not, would not believe?"

"Even one of My own will betray Me. It is the Spirit who gives eternal life. Human effort accomplishes nothing. The very words I will speak are spirit and life. But people can't come to Me unless the Father brings them."

Joseph sat shaking his head. "You will be betrayed."

"I will choose twelve to follow Me, but one will be a devil. He will abandon Me to a world that hates Me because I accuse it of sin and evil."

"What will become of You, my son? Don't spare me. I must know."

"I will eventually return to the One who sent Me. When they have lifted up the Son of Man on the cross, then they will realize that I speak what the Father taught Me."

"On the cross? I have spent my life working with wood and taught You the same, and You will be put to death in the Roman way?"

Jesus took Joseph's hand. "You asked. You insisted."

His father nodded, lip quivering. "Perhaps it is good that I will be gone."

"Religious leaders will call Me a blasphemer, for I will tell them that their ancestor Abraham rejoiced as he looked forward to My coming. He foresaw it and was glad. They will rail against Me, citing My youth, and demanding to know how I can say I have seen Abraham. I will tell them, 'The truth is, I existed before Abraham was even born.'"

Joseph's eyes shone. "You'll force them to kill You."

"They will be powerless until God wills it. I have come to judge the world. I have come to give sight to the blind and show those who think they see that they are blind. The Pharisees will ask if I am saying they are blind, and I will tell them, 'If you were blind, you wouldn't be guilty. But you remain guilty because you claim you can see.'"

"You will tell them, straight out, that You are the Messiah?"

"I will, and yet they will continue to ask. The

proof will be what I do in the name of My Father. But they will not believe Me because they are not part of My flock. My sheep recognize My voice. I know them, and they follow Me. I give them eternal life, and they will never perish. No one will snatch them away from Me, for My Father has given them to Me, and He is more powerful than anyone else. The Father and I are one."

Joseph hung his head. "And that is why they will put You to death? For blasphemy? Because they will see You as a mere man who has made Himself equal with God?"

Jesus embraced him. "You would have been a valuable disciple."

"I don't want You to die."

"But that is the very reason I am here! A kernel of wheat must be planted in the soil. Unless it dies, it will be alone—a single seed. But its death will produce many new kernels—a plentiful harvest of lives. Those who love their life in this world will lose it. Those who despise their life in this world will keep it for eternal life. When I am lifted up on the cross, I will draw everyone to Myself."

Joseph shivered and drew his cloak tighter. "It is such a heavy price. It pains me to think of You having to pay it."

"I want you to have My peace, Father. The peace I give is not like the peace the world gives. Don't be troubled or afraid. If you really love Me, you will be happy for Me, because I will go to the Father, who is greater than I am."

Joseph stood and moved away.

"Do you want to return to your bed?" Jesus said.

The old man shook his head. "I just hate to think of Your coming to such an end."

"Oh, Father, that is not the end! The rulers of this world would have no power over Me unless it was given them from above. And God will prove His majesty by raising Me from the dead after just three days! My followers will see Me briefly before I return to the Father. And I will send a comforter who will teach them and guide them in all things.

Take heart, because I will overcome the world."

Joseph sat again, leaning on his staff. "I do not understand all this. It is so foreign to me."

"It is not for you to understand. I tell you only to honor you."

"And Your mother? Will You tell her?"

Jesus looked down. "No."

"Will she be spared it?"

"No. She will witness much of it."

"Oh!"

"Father, God honored and blessed her by choosing her for this task, but sorrow will also attend it."

"I feel so powerless. My wife, my son, will suffer. And I will not be here . . ."

"You have been a wonderful father and husband. You, too, were God's choice."

The men sat in silence for a moment. Finally Jesus said, "Perhaps you regret wanting to know so much."

"No, no. In truth, I long to know even more. But I am tired. And I want to bless You."

"To bless Me?"

"May I?"

"Certainly. Father, I—"

Joseph used his staff to struggle to his feet and put a hand on his son. His voice was weak and quavery. "May the Lord bless and keep You," he said. "May the Lord make His face to shine upon You and give You peace. May He—"

And with that, Joseph pitched forward into Jesus' arms, his walking stick clattering to the ground. Jesus drew His father to Himself and bent to scoop him up as the old man's knees gave way. He cradled him like an infant and moved to the door, quietly calling out for His mother.

She rushed to the door and led Him to the bedroom where He laid His father on the bed, lowered His ear to the man's nose, then pressed His palm against the silent chest. It was all a show for Mary, for Jesus knew. He merely looked at her.

His mother's voice was thick. "I set aside fine linen and spices," she said, turning toward the door.

"Let Me go with you," Jesus said.

"I'm all right," she said. "I'll be right back."

And Jesus knelt by Joseph's bed, taking the carpenter's hand in His own. He lowered His head to the dead man's chest.

"Abba, Abba," He said, sobs invading His throat. "Abba."

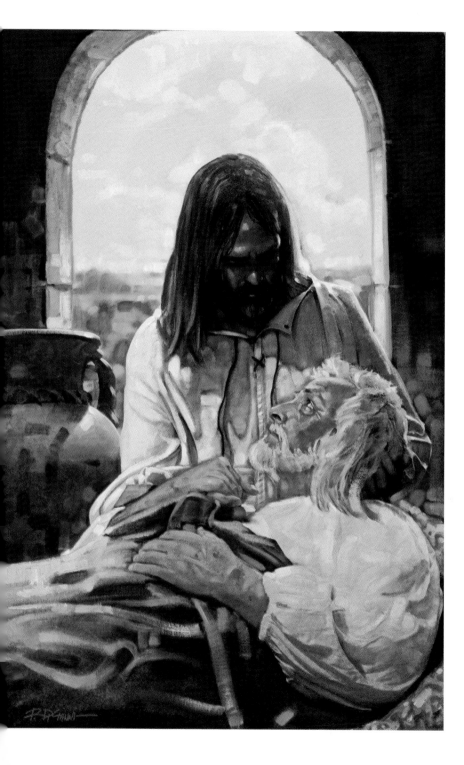